Eldridge J. Smith

Beautiful Builders

Eldridge J. Smith

Beautiful Builders

ISBN/EAN: 9783337417673

Printed in Europe, USA, Canada, Australia, Japan

Cover: Foto ©Andreas Hilbeck / pixelio.de

More available books at **www.hansebooks.com**

BEAUTIFUL BUILDERS,

BY

MRS. ELDRIDGE J. SMITH.

Afar down the isles of the misty past,
Away in the silence of years,
Were builders, who reared to the Living God
A temple, with prayers and tears.

NEW YORK:

HEARTHSTONE PUBLISHING COMPANY.

1886.

BEAUTIFUL BUILDERS.

I.

WHY do we not live as children of a loving Father? Are we aliens, and have no Father?

Why do we continue as children of sorrowing man, instead of God, our Father?

Why is it that we live amid darkness and despair, and continue saying, We are the children of God?

It is time that we soar away from our continuous theories, and acknowledge God to be our Father, Friend, and Brother.

It is time that we take our Father's hand and consecrate ourselves to life, and not to the fraudulent fever of theory—"the pestilence that walketh in darkness."

II.

THE fact of life proves our immortality, the Fatherhood of God, and the brotherhood of man, and the grand ultimate is, to love mercy, do justly, and walk humbly with God.

Ecstasy, fervent heat, and exhilaration are not Christianity.

These leave man, in the summer hours of life, listless. and without knowledge of his great inheritance.

We must be mindful of our ownership in Christ.

And we must keep our inheritance before us ; by this we will feel the influx of light, and the struggles through which we have come will be forgotten in the knowledge that TRUTH is ours.

And the desert of materiality will no more distress us, nor the sirocco of doubt parch us with thirst.

Let us, then, be of good cheer, knowing that our hands rest in the loving clasp of our Father.

Then we will fear no man, for the purity of soul gives Life, Truth, and Love.

We must cease wearing garments that give Truth the appearance of a living lie.

III.

Do we not hear, " We are sinners," continually repeated ?

Do these self-same accusers commit any less sin ?

Does the Father-God make mistakes, and leave them to be corrected by man ?

Does God the Father make a law, and leave the so-called sinner to make it over and hand it back to Him, saying, "This is your law revised " ?

No, this cannot be.

Jesus proves this, and said, " What I do ye shall do also, and greater works shall ye do."

The flowers of blessings innumerable that He gave are not asleep by the shores of Galilee and Genesareth ; these are ours to-day, for He says, " I am the same yesterday, to-day, and forever."

We know that Jesus blessed this glad earth, and " verily it shall be blessed."

We know that He left everything new and young.

And that all in His sight is as the sweet flowers of early spring.

IV.

LIFE is a golden harmony, but by adhering to darkness and despair we lose sight of our inheritance.

Amid human discontent we forget our lives are to grow as the lilies—" Consider the lilies of the field, they toil not, neither do they spin ; yet Solomon in all his glory was not arrayed like one of these."

We are thus made to understand that man is made in the " image and likeness " of God, his Father.

Thus out of self-imposed darkness we arise in the likeness of Him who says, " Come unto me all ye that are a-weary and heavy laden, and I will give you rest."

We realize that this gives us all things.

V.

LET us crave no more the deceiving light of every torch of theory.   Let us live in the kingdom of the Father, and be " taught as are the angels."

The " All-pervading" life gives us this power.

We are always dazzled by intellect, and unconsciously do honor thereto.

Thus, amid the strides of ambition and intellect, the wise soul feels self-poised, and rests in serenity, while the good deeds of the Master Christ become

as if they had not occurred even beside the shores
of Galilee, much less to extend to these hungry
mortals, to whom the crumbs falling from the
Master's table are denied, saying, "Christ's demonstrations were simply to show His power."

The perfect life of our Master gives evidence of
the power of Spirit over man-made theory.

And by His own words we know, if we do but
open our blind eyes, that the strength of Christ
belongs no more to the past than to the present.

It is now. "Now is the accepted time," as
much as it was in the ages ago, when the cry of the
lepers rent the air, " Tamé ! Tamé ! unclean ! unclean !" Jesus' heart instantly was touched, and
the lepers were cleansed.

Now is eternity !

The to-morrows and yesterdays are not ours, but
the Now is.

By looking on woes and misfortunes we weave
them for ourselves ; thus we cling to sin, sickness,
and death, finding no remedy except by the tortur-
ing theories of men, that go to great lengths to
prove that Jesus' practical life and teachings are
of no avail to us.

Let us spring to Light ; nothing can harm us,

and the Everlasting Galilee of Life is ours now, the grand eternal Now of God.

Theory and suppositions are like the sea, which bears its flower gardens on its upper waves.

By and by its treacherous rocks are felt, and the fleeting flowers are gone.

But Memory in the Everlasting Galilee of Life gives us constant joy, and we realize the meaning of, " These signs shall follow them that believe."

Upon our beings, mighty sea, let us tremble no longer, permitting self and ambition, with their paltry peace, to play upon our shores, defying our heart's yearning as the " Still Small Voice" says, " It is I, be not afraid."

VI.

LET us go forth and find love in God, " for God made man in His own image."

Let us prove our unity in Him by being the gladdest of all in the Bosom of the Universe, and give our lives no longer to self, but leap to the knowledge of our inheritance, full of the Spirit that makes us free.

Let us go onward as children of an honored

Father, knowing that the blessings of fortune and liberty are ours of Him—fortune in Christ's Life, and Liberty in His demonstrated acts.

Behold the grand life in the thousandfold love of all creation—the lion zealous for her young, the pelican baring her own breast, and nursing her young with her own heart's blood ; and will God do less to us ?

Shall we be forgotten or destroyed of God ?

Let us realize in our daily lives the beauty of our existence, and know this protection is ours of our Father.

Let us remember no impression is lost, and our daily lives are made up of these.

Let us bend our energies to have our lives accomplish better things than ambition's flattery, the which, as soon as its acme is attained, leaves us wounded and bleeding by the roadside.

We know theory cheats, but we know God will never desert us, nor drag us down to destruction.

VII.

WE say soul sins ; the Bible says, " The soul that sinneth, it shall die ;" now, does not this prove soul to be God's entity, for the soul is God's image, and "in Him we live and move and have our being." We could not do this if God had given us a sick and dying soul, for a sick and dying soul could not be God's image.

Mortality and Immortality cannot mix any more than water and oil.

We must gravitate toward God, as the earth does to the sun.

We must come to the Father, who gives us of Himself.

We must be transfigured from our theory-making selves, and know God's image is reflected in man.

We must approach our inner life, and ask ourselves if we are applying Christ to cure our errors.

Of what is all the world worth? The joy and pleasure that may be found therein is like all the knowledge the moon has of this earth—" her cold face sees it but by night."

We must reason ; behold, He says, " Come now, and let us reason together."

Remember, not one moment shall we admit God

to be the author of sin, sickness, or death ; we thus
lose all our conception of Him.

We must live gladly, divinely by the Spirit of
God—" Be ye perfect, as your Father in heaven is
perfect."

VIII.

As the days go by they admonish us to be like
God, for the spirit calls us all the while.

God and our Master Christ are one, and Christ
is our Brother ; therefore God is not different nor
distinct from us His children.   He gives to us His
Light, Life, and Tranquillity.

Life's hopes blossom in God ; let us wait for
them in His Light.

By this all pain will go out of life, and perfection
will take its place in the mosaic work of our existence.

Each act will have the care befitting it, each
thought will be content to grow in the sunshine of
the Life that comes of the Creator God, our
Father, " who giveth to all men liberally, and upbraideth not."

The Life that is ours is of God, and this being
so, we realize, " Be ye perfect, as your Father in
heaven is perfect."

Is man only the creature of an hour ! One short hour of life ! Is man the actor in all this his own created misery, sorrow, starvation, bitter pangs and woes ! Is he only the creation of himself ! Is he to be content in that short-lived rapture that comes of intercourse with his fellow-man !

Could this be so, he never could find himself again in the inheritance of God.

We must rally from our selfishness, and be linked in the Harmony of Life, and no longer dwell on the confines of a theory that cannot be demonstrated in the daily work of life. God makes our own by His own Life, and by the manifestations of the Life of Christ our Brother.

We are dazzled as children. We permit ourselves to be robbed by a theory that is powerless to give us peace by which to live, and we cry out, " O Lord, how long ?"

We must arise and trample out blossoms and fruits of wrong thinking—a thinking that will not demonstrate itself in comfort nor quiet, as " they that wait on the Lord shall mount with wings as eagles ; they shall run, and not be weary ; they shall walk, and not faint."

Let us not become impatient because the acorn of thought does not grow to an oak at once. Let us strive to bear in mind the flowering stalk and the full-grown ear, knowing their exquisite perfection comes of the finishing gold—" Be ye diligent in business, fervent in spirit, serving the Lord."

" These things ought ye to do, and not leave the other undone."

Man cannot be one without his Maker, nor will his Maker entangle him in snares and leave him helpless.

A proper father takes care of his children, and is God not as good ?

IX.

WE trembled at the serpent of wrong in our pathway, which God our Father never made.

We tremble doing right simply because we fear to do wrong. Let us strive to go forward and do right from principle, and thus realize we are at work in our " Father's Vineyard."

We are to remember Jesus broke no law of His Father in healing the sick and sending the message to us, " The works that I do, ye shall do also."

Remember, He says, " I and my Father are One."

Remember, He says, " All Mine are thine,"
" and ye are Christ's, and Christ is God ;" therefore, soul, thought comes back, and is precious in
the everlasting redeeming Motherhood of Christ,
the gift of God.

This God's best gift we do possess, without let or
hindrance, and with fragrant joy, as incense
breathing, we find Life and " feed beside the still
waters."

By our brilliant theories we spoil the life the
Master gives, and make our bread as bitter ashes.

Let us go forth in the strength of Life, and scatter
no longer toward heaven this self-thinking. Let
us arise from the thousand times ten thousand
theoretical decisions to the Giver, and drink the
divine Spirit.

Let us show forth Jesus' life, and no longer
tremble on the brink of traditions that demonstrate
not our loving Master.

For Jesus is our Brother ; less than this He is not.

And God is our Father ; less than this He is not.

Thus, side by side, " all ye are brethren," made
holy by the word of our Master.

In this heart-penetrating thrill we comprehend,

" He spake, and it was done ; stretch forth thine hand," and the hand was made whole as the other.

By this comes the comprehension of " Lazarus, come forth."

And we realize in this what is intended in the expression, " And the Lord buried him."

Let us, then, take the Canaan of eternal living in Christ, who gives the conscious knowledge of our thrice-transfigured existence.

X.

By reasoning as He tells us we will arise from the circumstances around us, knowing they are the acts of the present hour, and not the everlasting creations of the All-pervading Life.

Let us faithfully rescue every moment, and un-fetter our lives from spiritual poverty. Hath not God given us the delight of Himself, and are we, His children, not a joy to Him, and are we " making melody in our hearts to the Lord " ?

And we are His children before the world was known, for Jesus, our Friend and Brother, says, " Before Abraham was, I am."

God's love for us is as the everlasting ages.

Let us cease from wrath, however infinitesimal it may seem to us ; let us come no more into displeasures, but arise " to the mark of the prize, of the high calling of God in Christ Jesus."

Thus we will joyfully realize the Light of His demonstrated life, and gravitate toward the eternal Now of God.

XI.

To acknowledge that God makes death robs Him of purity, and leaves the impression that God beholds iniquity, while we should have it ever present in our thoughts, " God is too pure to behold iniquity."

XII.

THE goods of life are never appreciated, and we go on amid despondency, wondering why we have not more all the time. But our great overweening vanity and wrong prevents our giving the genuine test of good in every act, and keeps us from living in rich divinest love, and feeling that our lives are of God.

" For life is lived out of God," says the old German, Leopold Schafer.

Let our lives be sunny and bright. Let us stride away from all that wrests from us the golden kernels of the enwreathed grain in the Sunlight of God.

Our faces must shine of the life that is ours in pleasing beauty full of joy, and our daily lives prove that good is ever strewn with light ; and the more we share our gifts with others the more gladness and peace will come to us.

The power to exercise Life's tender sympathy is ever a welcome guest, and amid our selfish discontent paves the way to the acknowledgment of a privilege to reverence acts of kindness done in times of distressing need.

This privilege to dwell in reverence is our birthright of the Father.

This helps us share our lives with others, giving them a glad presence amid our bounty, knowing our lives are of God ; and this generous grace is reflected from man to man.

Without this joy life would be dark amid its selfishness.

Man in his wealth and power ofttimes forgets this essential of his being ; thinking not of others' wrongs and sufferings, his life is lived of poverty apart from the image of God.

Thus, out of his own discontent he lives and thinks that he has pleasure in his sense of taste, while he decorates his walls with art, of which his inner thoughts are ignorant, and covers his household in purple and fine linen.

2

It is the purple and fine linen of the life in God that is needed, and we must strive to attain unto it.

XIII.

As the little child throws its toys away and lies down on the grass asleep, glad in innocent joy, so must we cast out pride and wrong-doing, springing to the Life that is ours through inheritance from God.

Then will come joy and bliss, and "the beams out of the timbers shall answer it." This will bring the genuine Good, and "thy health shall spring forth speedily."

For out of this comes the divine living, "the only Life," and the image of God.

No play of human thought, no living, is Life but this—the right of living to God.

"Thy health shall spring forth speedily," knowing no power can deprive us of these exalted possessions; and we take of this glorified joy to help those who fall among the thieves of sin, sickness, and death.

XIV.

THUS man, a perfect whole, and God his Maker, and Jesus the Healer, Friend, and Brother, needs no act of tender pity to his brother to prove His Godhead.

XV.

THE deeds of ostentatious charity stir the stubble of thought; then men are pleased, and think that God is in this whirlwind of selfishness; but the " Still Small Voice" stands by at eventide, saying to the Adam of self, " Where art thou?"

Self, seeing only the whirlwind of its own creation, sits disconsolate amid the fragrant air and balmy sunshine, hearing not the "Still Small Voice," and continues striving to appease spirit-cravings with the chaff of its own oblivious undemonstrated happiness.

Thus self strides away amid its clarion of so-called charity, yet the " Still Small Voice " comes at eventide, telling us "Thou shalt have no other gods but me."

And the flaming sword of accusation, quivering in the horizon, makes man cry out, "I am more than the dust of annihilation."

And the Day Star of Hope arises in the sun-joyed sky. He says, " I will arise and go to my Father." Claim sorrow no more, but drink of the inexhaustible Fountain of Knowledge, God the Father, who says, " Come and drink."

" Ho, every one that thirsteth, come ye to the waters."

" Therefore shall ye draw waters out of the wells of salvation."

" Call upon His name, declare His doings among the people."

" For He saith, Are not my princes altogether kings ?"

XVI.

WE are sent onward in this present realm of being.

We know no more than babes.

For while we wait in the darkness of individual or self thought, striving to immerse spirituality into materiality—behold as we wait, the past, present, and future are absorbed by the eternal knowledge, " Now," and theory is eclipsed by the true conception of " Life, Truth, and Love."

And He walks with us to the resurrection of our being into the Israel of God, the Emmaus walk of Christ with us His brothers.

Then we realize the legions of evil go into the swine of theory, and are consumed in the waters of divine living.

Thus we come to the Light, and have the explanation of " work out your own salvation with fear and trembling."

For we tremble, knowing we have built our lives of human thought-material, evermore sunk into self and absorbed thereby.

But the wedding-train of Immortal Life eclipses the funereal darkness of theory ; thus we have our lives " hid with Christ in God."

XVII.

MAN cannot rob God. And we know man cannot rob us of Eternal Life.

Thus we stray no more, to be gone for years, to the enslavement of self.

Straying from Life's Eden, to be buried in a theory of man's creation, that ruins the morning of all our days, and makes the eventide, midnight and misfortune.

Straying from the House of God to the meritless positions of man, in his envious theories sculptured in sorrow, painted in pangs, by millions of mankind, waiting unfed in these unfruitful lands.

Searching these barren fields, our feet grow weary in the burning stubble.

But tenderly the Master of Life creates a new heaven and a new earth of our being, the sky of joy shines over us, making " life worth the living."

XVIII.

LET us " be diligent," and bear in mind that the ever-living God will aid us in whatever our hands find to do.

And in this blessing, we serve the day of life in honest duty, finding our worth in being glad to distribute of God's bounty.

And we realize what life is worth !

A new world forever hid with Christ in deeds of mercy, speeding all to happiness and blessings.

XIX.

BY this we find the Living Thought is ours, and we get a foretaste—" The half has never been told."

All life is crowned with Godhead's noble worth, and man, a part of God by Christ, our Brother, gives to us the place with Himself in the Israel of God.

When the lives we love go onward, and we feel without a friend, while the pale moon shines down as before, and the stars burn in the bright heavens, and earth, with thousands of children, goes gayly on as if to mock our woe, our hearts are bowed, and none can give comfort.

Behold the Finger writing in the sand !

The sand falls to its place !

The sea flows by !

The Master of Life waits ! And man, no longer, bowed by woe, goes calmly onward.

But he goes in hope.

Hope sprang to knowledge in Gethsemane !

And knowledge to peace in the Everlasting Pentecost of life.

But for this impervious well-spring of being that man is *co-existent* with God, our lives would be unbearable.

The demonstrated love in the life acts of the Master gives us peace and fills us with a perfect knowledge, and we go hopefully onward.

XX.

IT is humanity's inner life, the heaven of soul.

If thought has beginning, it has its end, " and

the glaring flash is all there is, and we to dust and ashes turn.''

But as we see the fact of being daily, it makes it less possible that it is a flash only made stronger by the strength its forerunner gives.

The Eternal joy is ours, or wherefore this longing for the Light?

Wherefore this thirst for purity?

Wherefore this star-eyed glory that shines back to our lives from the joy of childhood? And the soul-light that comes to us in our children's upturned faces?

Pure and sweet is the child-life and perfect is the soul won from self-thought ; and as the child-life unwittingly gazes on the beautiful, so do we brush aside the curtain which separates us from Life, Truth, and Love.

Does all this convey nothing but ashes? And has God given one swift moment and no more?

A world of beam !

A world of gloom !

A world of joy, to think, to feel, and all life's centre thrilled ! And then, to dust and ashes· turn?

O God, wherefore all this amid one dazzling day !   .

Life rushing back upon itself !

Itself destroyed !

And beauty, blessing, all for naught ! " Of His own will begat He us."

The Father hath to us His image given !

The Father !

The I AM !

And Jesus, our Brother, we were, and are ever with God the Living Light.

In silence and wonder we stand and gaze, and we feel safe as the stars above us, in the hollow of God's hand.

XXI.

THEORY gives to us the supposition that Nature lays her hand irresistible on bud and blossom, and on man, the prize of all !

Behold the coming of springtime bloom !

The circled earth !

The change of seasons one by one.   And year by

year, from childhood to the silver hue of time !
And all is turned to mould and dust !

Freedom and truth swept out of life !

Astonished at this giant stride, the heart goes to
its own funeral.

Remorse, with its sordid power, all the fond
memories has turned to ashes !

But the Spirit of Life, in the fair eternal Now of
God, gives back our heart's desire.

Thus amid this Spirit wealth we turn to our loving Father's heart and home.

And love abides !

And blessings in Life Immortal. And theory,
with its dust and ashes, sorrows us no more.

And we live.

And the Gospel of Love and Mercy is preached,
the deaf hear, and the weary find rest. Rest in
Jesus—*manifest life.*

Thus out of sickness we are well !

Out of sorrow we come to Light, and we do not
depend on material for eternal joy.

We spring to health !

We rest no more on doctrines and command-ments of men, and realize God did not make sin to tempt us, sickness to punish us, and death to make all life a blight.

XXII.

LIKE produces like.

We all know this.

And we know God is Life.

Can life produce death ?   Behold, He says, " Why will ye die, O house of Israel ?"

And since we know God is " Life, Truth, and Love," could He make death, when it also says, " God is too pure to behold iniquity" ?

Since Jesus our Saviour said, " Thy sins be for-given thee," did God make sickness ?

Could or would it be possible for Jesus to forgive Himself ?

Let us listen to the call, " Come now, and let us reason together," and inspire our lives with the power of the Holy Spirit, that leads us to all Truth.

By living so long in the thieving St. Giles of human thought our ideas are upside down.

XXIII.

LET us plead to ourselves of Truth as it is in our Master Christ.   Let us ever realize God as the only Author, and live outside of the scourge of theory.

For the Ladder of Eternal Life unites man with his Maker, '' who made all that was made, and all He made was good.''

Thus the whirlwind of theory will return to its source—nothing—and man, with '' the Still Small Voice,'' stand by the Bethlehem of Life and the Calvary of the Great Resurrection from self, to the living Master, the Redeemer from theory or human plans, to the living in Life, Truth, and Love.

Thus we will have the tranquil soul of heaven.

Thus whatever we purpose doing will be done as if in God's sight.

For whatever we may do is a part of memory to all lifetime, and the love of God will give to us His indwelling Spirit.

XXIV.

OUR daily lives should be a long reflection of good deeds done in pure good-will. And being done in love, we ask of man no thanks ; thus we possess the " Only Riches."

By having patience ourselves we command it in others, and hope and love come trooping in ten thousand times ten thousand.

And in this practice of all that is good we get the Father's image all the while.

We must therefore leave theory, and have the Spirit conception.

And when we see not the Spirit conception, we are apt to say our daily labor hinders our living Godward.

Are we not aware Jesus labored, and thus all our lives are blessed in it ?

We wander in the fields and behold the birds all about us full of song and praise, but do they not go down to the hay and stubble for food, and are they not the same ?

And are they not getting their living ? And in this labor the bird does not lose its identity.

And the clinging vines teach us as well to go onward in a glad gratitude to do whatsoever our hands may find.

And the Eternal Giver makes our lives natural in the recognition of His gift of Eternal Life.

By thus reasoning we go gladly onward.

We cannot be forsaken of God.   We breathe His breath as "He breathed on them the Holy Ghost;" this Christ gave to us, His brothers of right of birth, "and He breathed into his nostrils the breath of life."

"Behold all ye are brethren."   "And ye are Christ's, and Christ is God."

XXV.

MORE and more we see the healing of Jesus is ours to-day, or it was not by Bethlehem's hills nor Galilee's shore.

This gives to us treasures inexhaustible.

It numbers our hairs, and keeps us in the hollow of God's hand.

It gives us health, youth, and springtime bloom.

It blows from us the cloak that theory gave.

It unclasps the dross of greed.

It gives us the pristine strength of the baptism of birth.

Life prospers in its path, and sincerity is in its speech, for from the heart's "abundance the mouth speaketh."

We do know what we have seen, and do testify what we feel in our own lives every hour.

XXVI.

ALL things are taught to us of a past that God has blest, and we are left to a blind leading the blind present, that no God-power does bless ; and thus we linger in sorrow made by ourselves and sickness to which we cling, because no angel comes to stir the stagnant waters of our lives.

When life is open as a fountain, the birds drink at will, and why not the priest, teacher, friend, kinsman, and fair humanity combined ?

XXVII.

WE arose from years of illness, weakness, sorrow, and trouble by turning our lives to the "Real Living."

Many times we have been months confined to our bed. Many times have we supposed we had not long to stay in this life. Many times we have sorrowed over the passing out from the body of friends, tender loved ones, and of our heart's life, our own children, " and would not be comforted."

We all know words are poor consolation for wounded hearts.

Yet if you will notice, this is all poor humanity can give.

And why ?

Truly this is all it has of its poverty-stricken store, and can we blame any ?

Have we not often been told, " Is there no balm in Gilead ?" and the telling is all we can find out.

Thus we go on as before in our suffering state, seeking rest in the deluge of theory, finding no Ararat of mercy nor olive of peace.

And why ?

Let us think a moment.

By what power do we live ?

By what title do we speak of time as we measure each moment ?

Do we ever think a moment is the measure of our day ? And do we feel these to be precious, and that not one atom of what we are pleased to call time can we create? Yet we speak with authority of weeks, days, months, and years.

Do we ever think of their Author, and know He is ours as well?

"Come," says the Father, "and let us reason together."

The Father says, "Come now."

Come—now; behold, in this relation we are standing in the Light.

Could we reason with light and be in darkness when we address Light, the living God?

When we say, "Father, take my hand," He takes it, we go forth and demonstrate it in our daily lives, and if we are not better in bodily health and soul-life we have not asked of God, but our suppositional theory, and lords many, and gods many.

Sometimes we wonder any thought is attained, for man is left to suppose God's power only takes away sin, and that some other power is to take away sickness, its counterpart.

We adhere so to our human thinking that we find no meaning in the Scriptures as we read, "I am the God that healeth thee."

3

We are taught soul is immortal, and this immortality represents the Creator of all ; thus we feel we are made in the image of spirit, and Christ showing this spirit power, expressed the tenderness of motherhood as He wept over the Jerusalem of misfortunes and the Lazarus of distress.

And we the children of God should dwell in the acknowledgment of soul-power, and not give vent to paltry faith,—obscured joy, laggard hope, and meagre soul-research, ever standing alone, amid the catacombs of memory awaiting a voice to call us, when that voice is ours in the immortality of Life.

Man being God's child is hence like his Father, and the great principle in Christ.

Jesus, our God-man, supplements every human thought by His apparent physical suffering, and by His raising the sick proves Himself to be supplemented of God, and by His raising the dead proves Himself to be supplemented of Power, Principle, Life.

And by His raising His own body proves His supplementing life and immortality instead of human thinking and man-made doctrines ; thus man being His brother, and God our Father, and " I and My Father are one," gives to man his inheritance of Eternal Life.

He says, "Come now and let us reason to-gether," friend to friend ; by this we realize we are as He sees us, pure and holy ; in this way people feel the warmth of health return, and arise and walk, for all "Mine are thine, and all thine are Mine, and all ye are brethren."

If for one moment we could feel God sees us as He made us, we would feel the freedom of the free.

We must recognize our right to Life, Truth, and Love, and build up our barren lives thus, and see as Job, "Yea, in my flesh shall I see God, and mine eyes shall behold, and not another."

XXVIII.

"BE of good cheer, thy sins be forgiven thee," says the Master. Does this not show plainly that sickness, being sin, is not of God ?

Jesus would walk here to-day but for our deter-mining sin, sickness, and death to be a reality sent from God to punish us for wrongdoing. He says, "Arise and walk ;" let us take Him at His word, and walk toward Him, for lo ! He tells us, "I am of thy brethren the prophets."

Let us leave theoretical decisions behind us, and realize that He is breathing on us the principles we destroy in our blindness.

Let us awaken from our weakness in self, and

know He is " the substance of things hoped for," and by this will come to our lives the comfort of what Jesus means in the expression, " Before Abraham was I am."

This gives us our oneness with Christ, and the healing Mother Principle of Jesus makes God our Father.

We go on thinking of none of these things, but delve into all manner of ambitious desires, which deprive life of its early freshness, and bring to the eventide all manner of misfortunes.

Have we not this shown to us by the lives of our public men, gladly honored amid popularity, and soon forgotten when the sun of earthly greatness has set, and the bubble of grandeur gone out into poverty and disgrace?

But the flesh-pots of Egyptian darkness are hunted for by all, " And my people do not consider ;" therefore we seek to hear of sickness and distress.

Can we not strive to be as living souls, and not machines that grind out thankless, aimless lives?

Can we not give some evidence of the fruits of the Spirit? This we must do, or we are not a fruit-bearing fig-tree.

XXIX.

LET us cut down our many theories and arise to the "good part that shall not be taken away from us," the children of the most high God.

Yet our daily acknowledgment is, that we are the children of mortals, with an inheritance only of sin, sickness, and death.

We talk of "that Great Day" in which we shall give accounts of our thoughts, words, and actions.

We find the measure of that Great Day each hour, and we can fill it to none other than our Master's service, for God looketh on the children of men, "and He is too pure to behold iniquity." Hence only acts of purity and love can we offer to our Father.

And if we would look to God we "would be healed of all infirmities."

You may be ready to say, Tell us how?

Hearken! "None are so deaf as those who will not hear."

Look from the ordinary human standpoint to Jesus, our Friend and Brother. Can any sin or sickness be found in Him?

Now, in thus reasoning our lives to our Master we realize, "I am the God that healeth thee."

This is what the man did when Jesus said, "Stretch forth thine hand."

This is what the man did at the "beautiful gate of the temple," when Peter said, "Silver and gold have I none, but such as I have, give I thee."

The Light of Christ is seen by turning to Him, and we can do this as well as the lilies of the field that He tells us to consider.

"Not by might, not by power, but by My Spirit."

Now, if all these things could have been done to show His power only, what is left to us?

Let us go forward and bring forth the fruits of the Spirit, and we will realize that the life of Jesus in His great resurrective principles of Truth, Love, Mercy, and Perfection are ours to-day as well as when His hearers heard Him say, "These signs shall follow them that believe."

Let us go forward with our lives attuned to Love and Mercy, and we will realize, "Fear not, I am with you. Be not dismayed; I am thy God; I will strengthen thee."

He says come—now, not to-morrow, thus conveying to our lives an ever-present now; and this

He gave to us naturally by His love and tenderness.

So we have freely the life immortal of Christ, our Brother, who walked the wave, who said, "Suffer little children to come unto Me;" and every moment proves to us that He represents His grand harmonious life.

Let us cease binding our poor lives with the cordon of the world, in fear of every expression of man.

Let us sing the song of Life, and in our cradle-hours and our noon-day go forth full of joy and sing as the morning stars sang together.

"And the Spirit and the bride say, Come."

"And let him that heareth say, Come."

"And whosoever will, let him take the water of life freely."

XXX.

LIFE never was made to suffer; human theory does that plentifully.

We must work to rid ourselves of our preconceived ideas, and strive to know what is the meaning of "Truth, Love, and Mercy."

" God is no respecter of persons."

Behold, He sends Love to us, to show us of Himself, yet we see it not.

We want to realize these things, and in this " blessing" misfortunes dissolve by His Spirit.

And the clouds move away, giving us deeds of love in the place of human thought-material.

Amid the blinding wilderness of sin and misfortunes, in the midnight of heredity's gross errors we grope all our lives.

Yet we blame none. We wonder that we are able to go on even in this way. For we are supposed to be afraid of God, and only living what men call proper lives from fear of the world, and not from the Life-giving love of good.

XXXI.

Men insisting upon finding employment generally succeed.

We hunt every doctor's book and family traditions for names of ailments, and we get them. We tramp away down to our forefathers in a sort of pride, and claim a right of birth in all their diseases. We are rewarded abundantly.

We see our loved ones passing away with consumption in its almost worse than leprosy stages, amid its minutiæ of sorrow, and say these are the gift of Providence, and, being so, we have to unmurmuringly succumb.

And we see the horrifying results of these on every hand when Jesus, our Life, called sickness sin, when He said, " Thy sins be forgiven thee," and God our Father calls, saying, " I am the God that healeth thee."

Yet we ever are ready to say, Doctor So-and-so cured me last time, and I am going to him again.

And Doctor So-and-so is visited, and his remedies do not hit, and the poor targeted sufferer goes onward with the thorn in the flesh and the sick body, the body of death, ever his companion.

There is no need of this, or Jesus came in vain.

Yet you will say, " God made me to suffer, and I cannot get rid of it." If you were going across a field and a furious animal should start after you, would you try to run ?

Or would you, in your suppositional obedience, stand still, saying, " God placed this animal here to punish me, and I must submit" ?

Do you think you would have a moment's parley ?

Are not the wild beasts of sin, sickness, and death left to run riot in our midst, and no hand to pity and no arm to save?

Would a good father take a child and tell him to cross a field, knowing there was danger every step of the way?

If our common fatherhood and motherhood-love would not do this, how dare we thus accuse God?

How could the Great Creator give to us these things, since none of these attributes—sin, sorrow, darkness, and misery—are to be found in Him "with whom there is no variableness, nor shadow of turning"?

XXXII.

WE are the children of the Immortal God, or we are the children of nothing.

Immortality has no semblance of wrong! Mortality and the word lost, and the sorrows of life, belong only to our actions in the ever-recurring hour.

Could Immortality be lost, then God, the Author thereof, could be lost also.

We are to work out our own salvation from human stubbornness, that condemns what its daily life is ever committing.

What is the use of a profession that is only applied in theory?

Of what use is it when our lives are not even formed by its model?

We have to reason our lives back to our Father, whose arms are Love, whose Life is ours, whose Love is ours; and He gives us of His presence, "Lo! I am with you alway."

Thus Christ, our Friend and Brother, walks with us ever.

XXXIII.

GOD, our Father, begat us of His own will, and as He never can be lost, we cannot be. "Speak to the children of Israel, that they go forward."

Let us go forward, and leap to the Fountain of Living Waters.

He says, "Come and drink, and be full of the Spirit, and do justly, love mercy, and walk humbly with God."

We are the whisperings of God's Spirit, " made in His image."

Let us cling no longer to what history or tradition calls the Adamic living, but let us claim our birthright in the demonstrated life of our Master Christ.

Let us make rapid progress toward the Abrahamic purity in Christ, that sets us free from the slavery of sin, sickness, and the woes of death.

XXXIV.

By adhering to dead forms in our great perversity we see not the words of our Master, " Be ye perfect, as your Father in heaven is perfect.''

We must cease blotting out from our lives the transfiguration of Christ.

We should know our daily lives are to be made up of the purity of our Master.

Wherefore keep saying, I am saved by the blood of the Lamb and the Cross of Christ, stained with His precious blood.

Of what avail are all these sayings when our lives do not demonstrate the fruits of the Spirit—love, joy, longsuffering, gentleness, goodness, faith, meekness, temperance ; against such there is no law.

'' Not by might, nor by power, but by My Spirit, saith the Lord of hosts.''

" But the manifestation of the Spirit is given to every man, to profit withal."

" Now, there are diversities of gifts, but the same Spirit."

" And the disciples were filled with the Holy Ghost."

" And when He had called unto Him His disciples, He gave to them power against unclean spirits, to cast them out, and to heal all manner of diseases."

XXXV.

" Ask Me of things to come concerning my sons, and concerning the work of My hands command ye Me."

" Yet now be strong, ye people of the land. Yet now be strong, and be strong, all ye people of the land, saith the Lord, and work ; for I am with you, saith the Lord of hosts."

" The glory of this latter house shall be greater than the former, and in this place will I give peace, saith the Lord of hosts."

" I will cause the prophets and the unclean spirits to pass out of the land."

" They were troubled because there was no shepherd."

" I, saith the Lord, will be unto her a wall of fire round about, and will be the glory in the midst of her. And ye shall be a blessing ; fear not, but let your hands be strong."

" I am returned to Jerusalem with mercies."

" Blessed are ye that sow beside all waters, that send forth thither the ox and the ass."

" For then will I turn to the people a pure language, that they may all call on the name of the Lord, to serve Him with one consent."

" He hath shown thee, O man, what is good ; and what doth the Lord require of thee, but to do justly, love mercy, walk humbly with God."

" Seek ye Me, and ye shall live."

" Fear not, O land ; be glad and rejoice : for the Lord Himself will do greater things."

" I will ransom thee from the power of the grave."

" I will redeem thee from death."

" O death, I will be thy plagues ; I will be thy destruction."

" I have called thee by thy name."

" Thou art mine, I have redeemed thee."

" Before me there was no God formed, neither shall there be any after me. I, even I, am the Lord, and beside me there is no saviour. Remember ye not the former things, neither consider the things of old."

" I will ever make a way in the wilderness, and rivers in the desert."

" I, even I, am He that blotteth out thy transgressions for Mine own sake, and will not remember thy sins."

" For I will pour water on him that is thirsty."

" I am the first, and beside me there is no God."

" Even I will carry and deliver you."

" Can a woman forget her suckling child, that she should not have mercy on the son of her womb ? Yea, they may forget, yet will I not forget thee."

" Comfort ye, comfort ye, My people."

" O Lord, by these things men live, and in these things is the life of my spirit."

" Keep silence, keep silence, O islands ; and let the people renew their strength."

In all these expressions are Life and living God-ward told as plainly as is the every-day work of our lives.

But we attend more to visible observances of man than to the life-saving spiritual joy that is ours of the inheritance of God our Father, and therefore, when we feel out of health, we at once seek man and theory, still claiming life, when these only " make burdens that they themselves cannot lift with one of their fingers."

XXXVI.

WE are ever telling our beliefs.

Do we ever think of the real meaning of the word that so swiftly falls from our lips ?

To be constantly saying, " I believe ! I believe !" does not place us one whit nearer the accomplish-ment of life's work. · It is the knowledge of God our Father that we must have, and not a blind be-lief that demonstrates nothing.

" Seek ye Me, and ye shall live."

Let us hasten to this, and we will have our feet on the rungs of the ladder of divine living ; then the manifestations of the Spirit will be ours.

How ?

" Not by might, nor by power, but by My Spirit, saith the Lord of hosts."

The first thing to be done is to ask ourselves the question, Who am I ? And to clear up the house of our existence.

This is no idle task. It will take time and patience, and at once comes in the benefit of the " fruits of the Spirit." We will have much opposition, but we must be diligent and show forth fervent lifework in the vineyard. It makes no difference to the Vineyard Keeper at what time we commence, we shall all be equal. He says, " Shall I not do what I will with Mine own ?"

XXXVII.

WE want to realize our oneness with God.

Let us for a moment set all theoretical decisions aside.

Suppose you had a task of clearing sand from a large dwelling, would you not at once begin at the cellar, and would not the sand run from the upper part all the time until the last shovelful was thrown out ?

Thus we must continue throwing out the lees of sin, sickness, and death until we awake in His

4

likeness; and this we can do by Christ's own word.

Now, notice we are invited to the peace that comes of communion—" Come now, and let us reason together."

" Ask of Me things to come concerning My sons, and concerning the works of My hands command ye Me."

Now, suppose I simply ask the question, Who am I ?

Can you answer ?

If life extends no further to the life of God than the womb, then we are but dust and ashes of mortal man and mortal thought.

Whence came we ?

We do not know.

And only from a material standpoint can we answer.

Could any method of what we call science make the human body ?

No ; not even with all possible research could it make one hair of our head.

If we reason from a material basis we are lost in the marshes of theory and blindly go onward, saying we are the children of God, when we in nowise ever prove it.

What then ? " Stretch forth thine hand."

Who does that, we or the God-Life ? Can you answer ?

Since we know that it is not human power, it must be the God-Life ; thus our evanescent theories have to take wings, and we awake to the Sunlight of acknowledged Immortality.

Our daily lives are full of thankful joy as we realize there is a God and Father, and we His children acknowledged by His manifested life.

That there is a Creator who proves His Immortality and ours by demonstration, and gives to us this power in the daily act ; thus we are supplemented of Him in so doing.

We thus loosen the clasp of theory, and know the manifested life of Christ absorbs the Adamic principle and sets us free. Then we comprehend the words, " The glory of the latter house shall be greater than the former, and in this place I will give rest."

And we state God is a God of love and mercy

and vengeance, and repenteth Him of the evil, when we read, "I am not man that I should lie, neither am I the son of man, that I should repent." And we further state that Jesus' acts of mercy were for those times only.

Could this be so, what is left us but a supposition of life !

Can we take the tongue of truth to utter things impure ?

"Therewith bless we God, and therewith curse we men ; these things ought not so to be."

Now, we repeat, what have we left us ?

Behold a suffering body !

And no Christ principle to heal it. Behold our sorrow amid human thinking, and no mercy of immortality to supplement it.

Thus is it amazing that we cherish sickness as a friend.

Is it astonishing that we fear sin and yet clasp it in our every act and thought ?

Is it any wonder that we feel the sting and have a horror of death, and are groping all our lives in the midnight of sorrow ?

XXXVIII.

JUST as long as we seek life through death shall we grope amid the Adamic principles of fear, and the Noahic or Cheopian principle of the deluge of sorrow, running from the Eden of life in our material thinking.

We permit no mount of resurrection to shine down on the plains of theory, and "give rest in this place."

Some will be ready to say, "Of what use is all this? We are not able nor ready to cope with it." You will repeat to us, "All this blessing is only ours after we die."

"And that is what it can only mean, we die to go to heaven." May we ask at once, in reply, does it not say, "The kingdom of heaven is within you"? And the fruits of the Spirit are shown forth in the presence of heaven in the daily life.

But we wander on in our stiff-necked ways, and turn not to the Zoar of Peace, but cling to self, and stand a picture of life, encrusted with death.

And can life and death inhabit the same conditions?

And can truth, love, mercy, vengeance, sin, sickness, death, and hell come of one source?

Can these come of God—"God, who made all that was made, and all He made was good"?

What a condemnation comes to our lives by this thinking!

Behold, our friends fall into disgrace, we crush out what little lives they have left.

Our loved ones leave us for the grave, and our lives are made full of sorrows because of these errors.

We must go forth and recognize the power that came to the man with the withered hand.

Standing before our Master, we must strive to realize this power that Christ, our Brother, gives to us, and thus our depraved decisions will depart.

XXXIX.

BEHOLD our barren lives! "Teaching for doctrine the commandments of men."

"God said, Let there be light."

Let there be Light over this body of darkness. Breathe the inheritance that is ours and was ours before the Abrahamic hour.

" Before Abraham was, I am," and ye are Christ's, and the Christ principle and the Christ manifest is God.

" Wherefore bow your head like a bulrush ?"

" Seek ye Me, and ye shall live."

Drive off the Egypt of self, and the Spirit of Life will touch the waters of our lives, and " there shall be light." Thus theory gives place to Light, " and that which is perfect is come ;" thus we realize the tender Motherhood of Christ and the Fatherhood of God in the Love that is ours, in the entity of being, in the manifested principle, in Christ, our Brother.

Assertions are not-proofs.

We must go on to the work of our being.

Our conceptions must be " Life, Truth, and Love."

Daylight represents Christ, God.

The night pictures our own self-thinking in our theoretical lives.

We must grow to the realization that our Father sees us as He made us ; here we can see what is meant where it says, "Immediately he received his sight."

Thus we can heal our own lives and aid others to the knowledge, for as God only sees us pure, we learn of the manifest Christ in the pure and holy God.

This we should take in our lives as we do our daily bread.

But we make assertions that we do not comprehend.

Saying it is warm at the Equator does not make it so.

Saying all men are born free and equal does not make them so.

Never was there a more illy-used word than equality, for circumstances do make mankind very unequal.

We write voluminously on these subjects by assertion.

We rarely think of the unequal lives of mankind.

We see ourselves, and take for granted that the person who has less does not care for more ; and seeing people very poor, think that a little occasional charity is all they need.

So you see we carry our overshadowing selfish decisions in their despotic character to the needs of all living, thus severing life from demonstrating the fruits of the Spirit.

To demonstrate our ability to keep our faces to the principles of Christ and heal ourselves proves we are taking many steps toward God the Father.

And we find life so blest in the comprehension of the little we have, we thirst for more. And more is added, for the man who had five talents was increased, also one who had ten ; but the man with one talent went and hid his in fear.

To keep our lives toward God proves we hear the Master saying, '' I am the God that healeth thee,'' and '' The works that I do ye shall do also, and GREATER works shall ye do.''

This will give to us joy and courage in a grateful, peaceful life.

Let us persevere ; our Father is at the helm, and joy will come.

'' He that endures to the end, the same shall be saved.''

Saved from what?

A material living.

This salvation keeps us in health, and we see our lives demonstrating the great principles Christ's life explains.

XI.

THE principle of the orthodoxy of God is, Right Thinking.

The principles of the doctrines of human thinking is a whirlpool of misery and mystery by which to save a soul.

When but one moment spent in " Right Thinking " would close the seven vials of wrath and man know himself to be " a living soul."

Mere assertions are vain, but pure love gives life, and we are free with Christ in God.

Now we lock up all good in tiny earthly Jerusalem, inviting all the world to come to the shrine of self and worship.

We bring scorn and suffering with this dark material—thought, and feel self-satisfied, saying, " Lord, I thank Thee I am not as this publican, this unbeliever, who knows not the creed of man."

Let us cease talking of the intentions of the Creator, and get rid of the whited sepulchres full of dead men's bones, whose sickening odors make life a burden.

Let us cease cropping out in THEORY of the various plans of our Creator.

Remember, he who sits and makes plans and then retracts is not Immortal.

Behold how we do accuse God our Father! We thus make God appear helpless, and to get back to any feasible shape He had to do the best He could.

We thus make plentiful arguments by which God is to work to save us, His children.

Demonstration is what proves a principle. The entire creation is perfection, and a perfect God the Creator. And this perfect Creator is our Father; and that any circumstance of ours could hinder God is attributing to Perfection great imperfection.

That God intended having man pure, then to say He could not have man so, places God's acts on the plane with ours.

God calls us to reason, and we must know what Life is from the Demonstrator, and not from our perishing positions of thought.

Let us take Life for our Friend instead of the ceaseless thought of death.

Let us realize we are God's representatives, and that we are in concert with Him, and feel what Jesus says to be true, " Lo, I am with you alway."

XLI.

WE say to ourselves, How shall I prove this ?

The first point is to argue in our daily work, What is Life to us ?

Is God Life to us ?

Prove it.

Is God Love to us ?

Prove it.

Is God Truth to us ?

Prove it.

Now, at this point comes, " Work out your own salvation with fear and trembling."

It says " your own salvation," remember.

The beam has to come out of our own eye, and then we can see clearly to help our brother ; for the fruits of the Spirit in our own lives tells us what has become of our own traditions.

" And He said unto them, Full well ye reject the commandment of God, that ye may keep your own tradition."

Whether God is " Life, Truth, and Love " to us we can tell by the fruits of the Spirit ; and if these are ours we can comprehend, " what I do, ye shall do also."

And to produce the fruits of the Spirit is the raising our lives to the Life of joy, to feel, " O God, I thank Thee."

It is poor comfort to a sick person to say, " Bring forth the fruits of the Spirit, and you will be well."

The poor sufferer knows not of the life of Christ.

And we must remember our human thinking makes us appear a possible position of life en-crusted with death.

The sorrowing one will say, " For you to tell me God is Life, Truth, and Love ; then does all this misery come of Him ?"

Now we will tell you right here that we were at one time in this hour of anguish, and we went with quickening steps to one whom we thought a man of God ; he said, " Child, have you partaken of the Lord's Supper ?"

" Oh, yes," we replied.

" Well, are you not comforted ?"

" Comforted !   We are almost distracted to find some alleviation for our exceeding distress."

" Well," said the pastor, " if you can find no peace in the rites of religion, we have none other to offer."

We went away in a state that no language can describe.   We passed through a beautiful church, and as we did so we seemed to realize, " My God, my God, why hast Thou forsaken me ?"

In our great torture we went onward.   We thought there was no rest for us ; we were as the weary dove, no rest for the soles of our feet, and the deluge of man-made opinions hid from us the Olive-branch, Life.

In our exceeding distress we sought an aged man of God, one who had been many years in his Master's Vineyard, and who had long ago come to the " Life, Truth, and Love" of the Gospel of our Maker.

And soon we told our condition in as few words as the heart, bowed by its own misery, could utter.

The noble representative of God sat down beside us, saying, " Child, you are not to blame." He did not tell us the old story, to be patient.

No ; he had seen too many sufferers to tell them to be patient in a sorrow they could not combat.

He did none of these things.

But he said, " Seek God, the Life, yourself, dear child."

He poured into our lives the oil and wine of the Immortal Life ; God is Life, we His children, and the Father of Life gives not to us our sorrow.

We make it in our blindness, and in the terror of our lives no angel is near to place our feet in the pool of Living Waters, because our blind theories make a wall around us, and we will not look beyond, fearing that the customs of man may not approve.

Yet we hear people say, " All that is utter folly ; all of which you speak as being true was only done to show *Jesus' power as God*." We went home to our best beloved, and the prayer of Life, Truth, and Love that the aged man of God pointed to us went before us a pillar of fire by night and a shower of peace by day. And all our material misfortunes of illness and the shortcomings of

life were lifted, and the veil of the temple of
theory was rent in twain ; and peace, comfort,
and mercy came to our lives ; and now we continue
striving to polish the talents God has given us, and
more comes every hour.

We relate this simple incident to help yours and
our own lives all the time, for from our great material acceptance of life we are apt to let time wear
away the mercies that come to our lives in trials.

XLII.

LET us strive to remove selfishness from our
path, and show a perfect life in kindly deeds and
such like acts—making our judgment of our fellow-
creatures pure and not look of crime.

Redemption means release from bondage, and
Christ points to us the way.

And as God's breath is ours, we have this power.

Thus we realize God only sees us pure, and we
are redeemed from theoretically deciding on

What is Life ?

What is Truth ?

What is Love ?

Thus reasoning we have the release from sense, and come to the comprehension of every inclination of soul, with its modes, its opportunities and undiscovered abilities vested in the Power that never mocks nor trifles with us.

Thus the wonderful characteristics of Immortality absorb at once all insignia of sense, and Life shows forth its true Eternal Light in soul purpose and power.

And we come to the realization of our oneness with the Wisdom Spirit, the Triune Principle of Life which was and is. Thus with Love replete we feel the Master's words, and catch His tones in the music of His tenderness, as He said, "Our Father who art in heaven."

And He says, "Ask and ye shall receive."

Ask what?

Anything.

And we should ask, and know He heareth us by the witness of the Spirit that He hath given us.

It is in the absence of the Spirit that we grow weak, for "They that wait on the Lord shall run, and not be weary; they shall mount up with wings as eagles ; they shall walk, and not faint."

5

We seek not the Spirit, therefore we suffer and pass out of the sight of man, and the place of theory knows us no more, and we are called dead.

XLIII.

WE must remember that we can ask anything.

And we are to know, " no good thing will be withheld."

And what is more to the great work of life than health ?

We are to know God does not see flesh as sin. Behold, says Job, " Yet in my flesh shall I see God, and mine eyes shall see and not another."

Life is a blessing, but we stand afar off in our selfish lives, groping on in the darkness, and see it not. Now it says, " Take up your cross and follow Me ;" remember, it says your cross.

And whatever is our greatest weight, let us turn from it, and by the power that our Father gives, " these signs shall follow them that believe."

Then ye shall have health and strength of the Sunlight of God.

And there will follow the opening of the blind life and the raising of dry bones from the Jehoshaphat of theory to the walking, and leaping, and praising God for Life.

Now, how much time do we give to these things that are the " Only Life"? A few short words called prayer, hastily uttered, without any meaning or heart sincerity.

This is what most of us do.

Yet years are spent among the classics, and we thirst for more, thinking we have not half commenced the work we desire, while the great subject of Life is a sealed book to us, and we continue uttering a few words morning and evening, calling ourselves by the name of Christ, Christians, and when any one speaks to us on these things of God we think that they themselves are bereft of their senses and are in need of a physician.

The Great Physician is attended by our theoretical opinions, and is told, " Hitherto shalt thou come into our great phylacteries and temples, and no further."

Thus we go on.

And by and by the doctor and pastor stand by our bedside, and we ask, Is there no hope? The doctor and pastor are mystified.

They say the case is incurable.

They state how and at what time the trembling life shall pass out.

They then go down to their houses, or some similar scene.

But one of God's children, who knows the living God, and no longer permits fear or custom to defy the armies of the living God of the Israel of Life, comes in, and the weeping ones say, Is there nothing that can be done?

And they hear the words, " Look unto Me and live." And they hear the words, " Drive from your lives your selfishness ; let others live as well as yourselves, and the God of all Life shall give to your beloved one Life and Liberty ; Life in Christ, and Liberty in the free Mercy of that Life." Then all is quiet save the gentle breath of the loved one grasped from your selfish theory, and given back to your anguished life ; back to health, back to your home and your children.

This the doctors find in their coming (and they go away full of mystery as before).

Now, the knowledge that " the Spirit beareth witness to our spirit" should be studied as any branch of education.

That we are life and not death, and that we are

the children of life and not the property of man-made thinking and the terror of death—these are the things to study, these the object of living.

Why should not our children be instructed in these things as well as music, art, and literature? Thus preserve them from sorrow and a purposeless life, asking us, Is there no hope? and we as powerless by our blind lives as they.

Surely, if anything is attained by years given to music, art, and literature, we can attain at least as much of the study of Life by devoting years thereto.

And we must do this or our homes will be ever the pest-houses of misfortune, and no Samaritan of Life to pour in oil and wine.

We do know that mankind thirst for something other than suppositional theory, or we would not see the suffering ones break away from preconceived ideas and get off beds to which they have been confined for years, and are not afraid to tell the story that the Life of Christ, bearing witness to our spirit, has made them "free indeed." And the scorn and almost contempt lent by well-nigh all to whom these things are related is the cross to bear till the world awakens to the "Life hid with Christ in God."

XLIV.

WE do know that we seek release from sin, sickness, and the blight and terror of death. And yet if God sent sin to tempt us, sorrow and sickness to punish, and death to make all life a blight, by what right do we seek relief?

In fact, if God, the All Power, sends these to us, we have no right to ask release.

The very act of asking freedom from these would be in itself disobedience. Let us do as He tells us, " Come now, and let us reason together," and it must be from God to us, from Father to His children, and realize God our Father in the earth of body as in the heaven of soul.

And if we would reach the eternal understanding of Life, Truth, and Love, we must study the words of our Master, " These signs shall follow them that believe," with as much avidity as we do art, music, and literature.

Jesus healed the sick and put away error.

Was all this done to prove his God-being only?

Would the little attention that mankind paid Him make any amends for His physical suffering? Was it an example to us, and did He say, " The works that I do, ye shall do also, and greater works than these," only to be applied to that time.

By His telling us, " Greater works than I do shall ye do also," Jesus showed forth the fruits of the Spirit, thus giving our daily lives strength.

We must cease to arrange for God our Father from our erring standpoint, and this will help us comprehend, " I am the Way, the Truth, and the Life," and will aid us to cease judging the motives and acts of our fellow-mortals.

XLV.

WE must represent Life, or the coming of Jesus was in vain.

We can in nowise be life encrusted with death.

For Life is God, and in " Him is no variableness nor shadow of turning."

We ask ourselves, How are we to attain the witness of the Spirit ?

" The seed is in itself."

God sees us as He made us, or there is no salvation, for God is pure, and hence has not seen us.

We are so peculiarly tempered that we never see the beam in our own eye.

The witness of the Spirit comes to us in demonstration.

Harmony is the kingdom of heaven, and the opposite brings to our lives all misfortune.

It is every one's duty to make life cheerful and bright.

It is our privilege, given of the birthright of God, and our homes should be perfect types of the heaven of soul.

You are ready to say, "And how can these things be, when we have so many annoying duties?"

Herein is the showing forth the fruits of the Spirit—"meekness, temperance, and not rendering railing for railing, but, contrariwise, blessing."

This we can do, and we should hasten to its accomplishment.

We should make it a part of the business of life to have our surroundings such as keep us Godward. Burdens and hardships are thus lightened, and we gladly bear them in an atmosphere of love, as the people on shipboard keep cheerful in a storm when they, the captain, and crew are in harmony.

Mankind is wrestling to be rid of the night of inharmony.

The genuine type of harmony is the manifestations of the " fruits of the Spirit."

We must hasten to the Siloam of Life.

We must not linger in the Gomorrah of man-
made theories, amid the Lot of indiscretion, but
flee to the Zoar of Hope.

We are all in Christ's care, for He says, " I am
thine, thou art Mine," and the heaven declares the
glory of mind, and the firmament of body showeth
forth His handiwork.

XLVI.

MAN's chronology is " by and by."   Man always
leads a life of unrest, putting off for a coming
time, ever saying, " By and by."

God's chronology is Now.   He says, " Come
now."

" Now is the accepted time."

This gives peace and life.

And the wayfaring man need not err therein.
The wayfaring man comes quietly along the road,
he thinks not of fear, he knows the King's Highway is ever in order, so that his footsteps shall not

slide, and he goes calmly onward in the Peace the King's Highway gives him.

Let us strive to cease living amid a theory of woe that God has not given, and ask ourselves often, Whence cometh Life? Thus seek the knowledge of God and Jesus, whom He has sent.

Searching creation, we find man the only object of misery and unhappiness.

And he proves it daily by looking on life from an unholy, theoretical standpoint.

Fathers and mothers labor, the children around them are not taught the aim of life, and they all drag onward, only studying evanescent pleasures.

This makes children appreciate nothing; their lives are spent in a whirlpool of wasted time, the real meaning of home is lost, and the ring of empty vases is all there is left.

The child is only seen from the theory-limiting life of the parents, but we should know God is Life in the great depths of the yearning Love Eternal.

God is Light, and His reflection is on all.

Man talks of death so constantly his thoughts take up the resound; and thus continuously conversing of the sorrows of life, stands ever in dread of them.

Life weds not death.

God gives to us great riches, but we see them not.

Thus we turn away from the call, " Come now, and let us reason together."

Jesus, taking up His own body, proves to us the soul forever has a body, and can no more be separate than we would suppose a man to walk without his legs.

We do not wonder that what is called death looks so terrible, as we assert the soul is torn from the body, God having to destroy His own work to get soul from body.

Let us start forward with an earnest determination to get away from this frightful slough of irritating misery that drags us in chains and darkness.

Let us leave doubting far behind, claim the inheritance that is ours, and take the coming of our Master as He demonstrated it.

Is it not time to awaken from our lethargy, have God for our Life, God for our Friend, let go wrath, let go displeasure, and thus put away the heathen gods which we worship—the gods of self and pride ?

How absurd are many of our acts and words !

We say, Yes, yes, I believe in Jesus, but you know Jesus did not mean what He said, for we have no explanation " that these signs shall follow them that believe."

XLVII.

Now, it would appear that from our various strifes and emulations the place called the other world was of no importance to us.

We act as if this life could be of no use either, as it is only spent in making misery, while we waste in our hard-hearted luxury abundant means, knowing many of our fellow-mortals have not the necessaries of life.

We should see that such living cannot demonstrate the fruits of the Spirit.

We make great outcry as to the breaking of law, yet we have everything in our lives before the study of God our Father, who is our Life.

And of what use are such lives ?

Does this manner of spending the precious moments lengthen our life ?

Does it make a grand usefulness come to all ?

Is life better for greed ?

Does it not make long furrows in the face, and longer ones in the heart ?

Thus the family comes up in a lazy idleness, perfectly ignorant of the earnest duty of life.

Is life more a state of mercy than joy ?

Let us seek to win soul from sense and live in the perfect Life.

And does he not spend his life to enlarge wealth, and does he yearn for the Light of Life as well ?

Does he not grasp wealth, that totters with him to a sour old age ; and if this stage is not attained he drops, amid the freshness of his manhood, into a grave of his own making, full of disappointment and despair.

XLVIII.

GOD's creed to man is Life, Truth, and Love.

It is wafted to us from our every conception of a merciful Creator, " who forgiveth all thy iniquities, who healeth all thy diseases."

Yet behold the way in which we reverse this.

We may read all history, and we will find mankind drinking in sorrow and calling to life no light nor peace.

Man goes on all the time as if there could be no other creator than himself.

And his acts are as if he had no other thoughts in life but to make money and linger out a cross, soured existence.

But his name should be in the hearts of the sorrowing amid divinest loving memories that come from the soul-life of good, in the living he should have to God.

Jesus, the Friend of man, showed us a model of life, but we go onward as if He had purposely said, "I tell you these things, but I know beforehand that you will not do them."

Now, if any one would tell you that you do not believe in Jesus you would make one assertion on another, saying, What do you mean?

Behold, the followers of the pure and holy Master must demonstrate the fruits of the Spirit.

They must be free from pride and hard-heartedness.

They must be free from malice and all ungodliness. These come of the pride of life, intellect ; and this is absorbed in itself instead of the grand conception of Jesus, our Brother.

We have enough sorrows and misfortunes to be surfeited of self.

And that which brings nothing in its train but sickness, sin, and death needs our earnest attention to hasten to destroy and awaken to the demonstrated Life of the real living.

The Master's way is plain, but we go onward, always talking of the hidden mysteries of God and His Gospel, when He who is the Gospel to man His brother says, " And a little child shall lead them."

Do children lead to hidden mysteries ?

Behold what our Master says plainly, " Except ye become as little children," thus showing that the simple trust of children brings us the " new birth."

XLIX.

" YE must be born again " of water and the Purity of Peace.

This makes us strong in our daily living.

When we cease wrong acts, then we are done

therewith ; thus comes forgiveness, for we are not forgiven in the continuance of wrong.

We cannot have an Ananias peace ; the whole life must be right.

By leaving all disturbing elements out of life we seek the Kingdom of Harmony.

Thus " we find the peace that passeth all understanding," and begin to get the conception of " ye must be born again."

Thus we see the Immortal, and come to the new birth that is ordinarily called " conversion."

Thus we comprehend the life-giving words, " Son, give Me thine heart."

Heart being in the centre of the body, and the representation being perfect to us, we then have some conception of its meaning, and have some idea of our Creator God, and the words of Jesus, as He says, " Go, preach My Gospel," " go, heal the sick," " cast out devils," " freely ye have received, freely give."

Yet theory tells us these things were for that time only, and were only to show forth His power as God.

Now, if these things were only to show His

power, the teaching is vain, and we have but to cling to material statistics, that kill more often than they cure.

Thus we see how theoretical decisions fill all ages with sorrow.

And a life demonstrating not the fruits of the Spirit is bowed in misery while it talks of proclaiming the " acceptable year of the Lord."

" Come now, and let us reason together."

We are made in God's image, and this takes from us every form of wrong by the inexhaustible Life-Fountain, the Christ-Principle, the Christ-Life.

Sin and iniquity cannot abide in Immortality, and we see not the I, but the sin. We see not I, " the image and likeness of God," but the daily determining of sin, sickness, and sorrow.

We must grow to the realization of the Spirit, and know sin and Immortality cannot mix, though our theories make them appear to be clothed with Life.

L.

BEHOLD the glove on your hand, it is but a covering woven for its use ; thus see how we make all life appear what it is not by our suppositions, that would engulf the " Soul Immortal."

6

But with all these things before us we have to
reason our lives back to God and know He is our
Father, and Jesus our Brother, who was with God
before " the world was."

Thus, being co-eternal with God by Jesus, our
Brother, we cannot be harmed, for " He breathed
on them the Holy Spirit, and Spirit* is substance,
and God is the substance of things hoped for."

Are we not laboring to destroy sin and sorrow ?

Could we be able to do this if they came of the
Immortal God ?

As we give up our hold upon sin it leaves us.

Jesus showed us the way, and we must " follow
on to know the Lord."   And we are to have life-
giving proof in all our acts, for He says, " Be ye
perfect, as your Father in heaven is perfect."

LI.

LET us take the outstretched hand of Mercy, our
Father, and know the ever-living freedom is ours.

Behold the words of comfort.

" Ho, every one that thirsteth, come ye to the
waters, and he that hath no money ; come ye, buy,

and eat ; yea, come, buy wine and milk without money and without price." Thus we are taught of Mercy, and the clinging remnants of past theories drift away.

Let us build up our lives by our Master, and we will keep in the pathway of Life.

We will come to the comprehension of " Bring no more vain oblations ; the new moons and the Sabbaths, the calling of assemblies, I cannot away with ; even the solemn assemblies. Your new moons and your solemn assemblies my soul hateth."

LII.

THE way in which lives are spent, is it singular people cry out when we say, " These signs shall follow them that believe" ?

Is it astounding that life has the aspect of mis-fortune when we are so hard-hearted ?

Let us hasten to claim our title in Life, the Israel of God.

And let us know the Zion of existence is ours, for He says, " I will place salvation in Zion." Let us realize the world around us is claiming its in-heritance in the Comforter, who sends us blessings innumerable ; but our selfishness hides them from our eyes.

Why is it we seek sorrow, when creation is so jubilant with joy ?

Most teaching makes us feel ourselves a sort of nonentity made to be cursed, and yet urging our claim to the entity of God our Life, as we all know entity is the substance thereof, and " God is the substance of things hoped for."

Behold, Jesus' mission on earth was to show man and his Maker to be one, for He says, " All ye are brethren, and ye are Christ's, and Christ is God."

We must arise from our lethargy and be real shepherds, gather the sorrowing from the east and the west, and sit down with them in the blessing of Life, Truth, and Love.

Yet both teacher and pupil go on in a dull agreement that demonstrates only sin, sickness, and death.

LIII.

Is it not time that the waste places blossom as the rose ? Is it not time that the war of words cease, and the knowledge of the demonstration of the fruits of the Spirit should occupy our lives, gather the hungry from the wayside, feeding them on Life, Truth, and Love, instead of the husks of materiality, which involve us in desolation ? Let us seek the shepherds that wait on the Lord, and no longer wander from our Father's House.

Men are very careful in every avenue of business to obtain faithful superintendents and machinists, who give demonstrations of what they can do by the perfect work they produce.

Yet guardians, teachers, and preachers are taken and are given us daily who do none of these things in the demonstration of the Spirit, that is to " profit withal."

We are said to have a decaying body encasing an immortal soul. And after this impossibility is gotten into the world, this so-called condemned criminal is said to be here to praise God and to show forth His power. Then the thing called man, this life and death mixed, is to praise Life, that is God.

The accused praising the accuser, the poor unfortunate criminal, man, praising the ever-present God.

The so-called miserable sinner, man, the representer of death, praising Life. Then some of these singularly unfortunate criminals, without any regard to their state, are damned, and some are saved.

This would not be done by idiot judges among these self-same criminals.

Yet behold how liberally we accuse God, our Creator, of these things to His own children, made " in His image."

God must be Life and Purity, and we, His off-spring, must be of His own forming.

We cannot represent life and death, when He says, " O death, I will be thy plagues !"   " O death, where is thy sting ?   O grave, where is thy victory?"   " Why will ye die, O house of Israel ? And I take no pleasure in the death of him that dieth."

When we see a person spend a long life of good, and then see them afraid to go to the Master upon whom they say they have been waiting, this gives us new thought.

LIV.

WE speak of the Bible as a precious treasure. We make it " ours" only as a man who owns a fair field, with streams and running brooks that would turn millions of mills to give work to mankind, but he, looking on, says, " Thou art mine," and know-ing of the River of Life, gets no blessing himself, and hinders others.

We would not spend so much time telling our children to do work that we, by our great supe-riority of judgment, knew they could not nor would not perform.

Thus we accuse God our Father and Jesus our Brother of doing that for which we would turn a man out of the community.

The more we hearken to the call, " Come now, and let us reason together," the more we have the Perfect presence in all we see ; and the less we say and think of sin and its hold on man, the sooner will come to us the Peace of the Perfect man in Christ Jesus.

The fact of Life is in the existence of God, and this was manifested in Jesus ; and it is daily made plainer to our lives that God is Light.

And from Light there goes no darkness.

And from Truth there comes no wrong.

Every hour brings its care and duties, and there is no discharge therefrom ; by striving to see clearly these things, we find our lives grow more strengthened, and we begin to feel indeed our " Father is at the helm."

Joy in labor and Life to aid in the pursuit.

God to crown all, making us a unit in Himself.

LV.

God rolls the stone from the sepulchre, and we see plainly the Master, Friend, and Brother.

We must be diligent.

The entire creation tells us there is no idleness
in our Master's Vineyard, and in this the thought
of sin shall perish of itself.

So long as we stray in the inheritance of sin we
will hold to it.

We, being God's children, are the inheritors of
light. The more we study the Word, there comes
to us, "I am thine," and by the knowledge that
we are the substance, the entity of God, we are
well.

And it is in the entity or substance of thought
that we use the appellations Supreme Being, Orig-
inator of all, thus meaning God. Appellation
meaning the name of an object, and entity ex-
pressing the " substance thereof."

" And Christ, God, the substance of things hoped
for."

If we would closely behold our expressions and
reason with ourselves, we would see that we attrib-
ute to God acts of which we would not accuse our
fellow-creatures.

We never think that we are privileged to come

out of these rock-bound caves of superstition and spring to Light.

We make laws that we ourselves will not touch with one of our fingers toward giving them to our fellow-man, knowing well he would not hearken thereto ; yet we call these things God's laws.

But we do this in poverty of thought, as our lives are not in the demonstration of the Master.

By these things all creation appears in chains to us.

All things come to us of the ancient traditions, while we are struggling unconsciously for the Light.

Groping for the Light, we dwell in fear of some man-made customs that hinder us in the good we yearn to do.

But amid our cowardice we go toiling on in the meshes, striving " to serve God and mammon."

Oh, what a condemnation this is to us, as well as to our teachers !

Have we to toil on and feel this fear of what our fellow-creatures will say of our testimony for God ?

Are those who have been made free from sin and sickness, its counterpart, to keep silent ?

Are those who know the ever-present God to be their Life to be kept silent, fearing they will not be believed?

Did Jesus' own disciples believe Mary when she said, "The Lord has arisen"?

And shall we permit the thieves of theory to rob us of our trust, and find no Samaritan of Life to heal our wounds?

Are we to be silenced by fear of men and their laws?

And does it not say the fruits of the Spirit are these—"love, joy, longsuffering, gentleness, goodness, faith, meekness, temperance"? Against such there is no law.

LVI.

THUS we are set at liberty by the Gospel of our Master.

We have seen persons for years have every symptom of consumption, and be told by the doctors that their lungs were in a very bad way, recover by realizing Life to be God, and that Life, the gift of God to us, is the birthright of man in the Mind of Jesus.

And we do know that these persons go out and in among us, full of joy and strength.

For God has healed their thoughts from a determination to suffer as a part of the inheritance of man, and their lives grow in the knowledge of walking and leaping and praising God, and they are "diligent in business, fervent in spirit, serving the Lord."

Many are the cases of healing; is it all nothing?

If it is of man it will come to naught, and it is time that the scoffers should come forward and prove it to be nothing.

We who have laid on beds of agony for weeks, months, days, and years, do we not know there is a balm in Gilead? And are we to be silenced for fear of what man may say of us?

Jesus says, "Come unto Me all ye that labor and are heavy laden, and ye shall find rest," and we will take Him at His word.

We have seen the mind in distress comforted by realizing, "These leaves are for the healing of the nations;" and we have seen persons ill with fever, and have heard them say, "Master, we are in your image, and surely this fever never came from you."

Then we have known a sweet sleep during which the release came, and the sufferer awakened completely restored.

Thus the heart is full of joy without words, the pale, worn look goes out in the swine of sin that gave it its power, the face shines as the morning, the tardy footsteps grow light, and the life shines out of God, whom it represents.

We can bring a cloud of witnesses to attest these facts in our lives and those of others.

We know of homes where the ill-tempers of the inmates have become quiet by finding God to be Love and Mercy.

LVII.

BEHOLD, the healing Master says, "I am the same yesterday, to-day, and forever." Behold, He says, "Ask in faith, nothing wavering."

This is Life, and it is not far away, but here in our midst, for He says, "The kingdom of heaven is within you."

LVIII.

WE cannot create Light from darkness; Time keeps us thinking that joy has to be postponed to a "by and by," the foretaste of which the life shows not.

Time is only cognizant of these circumstances of misery.

Out of time there is no wrong. We prove this

by the Immortal Life that calls us, saying, "Come unto Me all ye that labor, and ye shall find rest."

The perfect peace of the Immortal has no time nor wrong.

LIX.

WE have read each day for years, "Blessed are those whose iniquities are forgiven, and whose sins are covered." "Blessed is the man to whom the Lord hath not imputed sin, and in whose spirit there is no guile."

And then, "Thy sins and iniquities I will remember no more."

Now, God being no respecter of persons, there could be no such thing as blessing some and cursing others ; therefore, God, "being too pure to behold iniquity," is the Author of blessings only.

"A good fountain sendeth not forth sweet and bitter waters."

And if our daily duties could be analyzed, they would give joy and strength instead of constant weariness.

We must keep out of sight the flaming sword of theory.

LX.

THIS theoretical sense of things makes life appear to us first an outlook of pain and then pleasure, both from the same source.

That would be looked upon as impossible in anything except our own lives.

If we were going abroad the subject would occupy our minds, and we would make investigations as to the journey.

Eternal Life surely is of more value than any journeying, and we must commence to day to give it consideration.

Scripture says, " The tops of the highest mountains appeared.''

Why not take this to our lives, and the tops of the mountains of Life will arise, and the floods of self; sin, and darkness will disappear.

We can no more find the eternal living by chance than we can pick up our daily food in the streets.

LXI.

As the waters chase each other to the shore while the steamer ploughs the waves out of their course, so does our material thinking rush from our pathway at sight of Love and Mercy, and the " King of Glory comes in.''

Yet there comes back to us one and another of these material ripples ; thus our quiet is disturbed ; by this we can realize the fig-tree withering in its barrenness, and we hasten to the Meribah of Truth, lave our lives in the Sea of Life, and materiality gives place to the Presence of our Master.

LXII.

WE must remember the holocaust of sin and wrong is just as unnatural as is war, and we must arise in the power of the Life that is ours to depart therefrom.

We are able, in the strength of our God-being, to work out our salvation from the body of this death, and walk by the Living Waters, hang our harps material on the willows of weakness, and take from the Tree of Life the Golden Harp, " that ye do justly, love mercy, walk humbly with God."

We are by no means at work to help ourselves ; we delegate our thinking to others, and go on in sorrow.

Clear out the money changers of self, and the " King of Glory shall come in."

And when we shall lay these unclean things aside, we shall receive the blessing of His salvation.

LXIII.

WE have to lead a noble life to show forth the fruits of the Spirit.

The reason we see men so indifferent is that all things holy are regarded a mystery.

Let us attune our lives to Love, go forth gladly to labor, bearing our sheaves with us in the already demonstrated life of Christ.

Thus being in prayer full of the knowledge that we are made in God's image, we are whole and happy. Let us take Jesus at His word, as did the man with the withered hand.

Thus the chaff theoretical must flee away ; then comes the baptism of Light, that opens the blind eyes.

LXIV.

Now men make deductions from the past as precedent for the present and future.

People criticise and listen.

Newspapers copy, and the scientific world judges and accepts.

Then can we not take the like and have our Master's work now, and render to Life the respect we give to theory ?

LXV.

LIFE is either a theory of man or a reality of our Maker.

It must be decidedly one or the other.

By making suffering an entailed estate we are cheated of our birthright.

Let us read our Bibles, digesting the words for our souls and bodies as one in the Master. Thus reasoning, the Bible is of unspeakable comfort.

Thus the Eden of Life is ours, and the desert blossoms as the rose.

LXVI.

" WHO is wise, and shall understand these things prudent, and ye shall know them ?"

Now, let us decide, Is the peace of Christ the desire of our lives ?

Can the great thirst be of mechanical origin ?

Can it be a passion ?

Can it be only enthusiasm ?

7

Or is it but a momentary observance of forms ?

All of these things we have to decide by bringing forth the fruits of the Spirit.

Let us cease eating the dependent bread of theory, with its scrambles for evanescent earth-born power.

Let the vats overflow with the wine of Love and Mercy.

A right living we inherit of our Father.

We must launch out in the deep, and help the helpless.

There are many of us who from our early child-hood have been members of a church, yet our lives have not corresponded with our profession.

And it is life but in name, a sepulchre full of sickness, sin, and death.

These things should be the object and subject of our lives.

Let " us consider the lilies of the field, how they grow."

How do they grow ?

By living a natural lily-life—free, simple, and natural.

LXVII.

WE rarely think of the misery which we may inflict on others until some occasion crushes our foot against the inevitable wall of self ; then we open our eyes to Life, seeing others have a right also.

It is the realization of Life that gives man power to help himself.

LXVIII.

THE yesterdays of clouds harm not to-day's sunshine ; neither can any act of man mar the Life Immortal.

The Book of God is mapped out in the creation around us.

Yet we unwittingly gaze, gathering shells material, and as unwittingly throw them one by one away.

Yet we keep the Father's image, and if the scales lent by theory material could fall, we would then see the " lilies as they grow."

LXIX.

WILL man be so forgetful of his life-labor as to curse it ?

Will a loving mother, looking on her deformed child, curse it ?

Think ye, then, God curses us and makes us
slaves to sin as a part of the so-called human
nature we inhabit ?

We must overcome the Adam and Eve of thought
in determining against sin, and thus be relieved of
the weight that besets us.

We do know a loving mother most tenderly
loves the deformed child, seeing not its condition ;
and is God less or less good ?

Legions of evil cannot bind us to sin ; we are the
offspring of the Life that is God.

Then, on to duty !

Love sends us at every heart-thrill its message of
Life, yet we turn away, saying, " I am holier than
thou." But the Voice of Free Grace cries, " Escape
to the Mountain," and the Waters of Life's Fountain flow freely to all.

LXX.

WE talk so much of sin and iniquity that it en-
velops us as night. We must free ourselves, and
" open the year of release to all generations."

We marvel no more at the lives of men, for instead of finding quiet and comfort in the every-day

life possessions, man chains himself thereto, forgetting their uses.

Thus no one sees any farther than the taskmaster custom, which comes, an unwelcome guest, robbing us of our peace.

LXXI.

HARDNESS of heart cannot give joy, yet people grasp it as dearly as life.

We do not acknowledge blessing, or our lives would be less suffering, and our acts more just.

Yet we drag on, making work a burden, seeing not the sheltering life of Christ, as He wept over Jerusalem.

"O Jerusalem, thou that killest the prophets, and stonest them that are sent unto thee, how would I have gathered thee as a hen does her chickens under her wings, and ye would not."

LXXII.

IT requires time to learn anything. And how much do we give to spiritual subjects?

To get man to this study is no idle task.

By acknowledging theory has power leaves us helpless.

Thus we take away from our lives the conception of God.

Behold, we are ever talking of prayer ! Do we think of its real meaning ?

And to pray is to draw nigh to God in any way from which we get the most peace.

No one can teach us how to pray but the Master, who said, " After this manner pray ye, Our Father, who art in heaven, give us this day our daily bread."

This is Jesus' benediction to us, and is ratified in the Evening of Memory, as He sat there blessing our lives, saying, " Do this in memory of Me ;" and this is borne out in acts of mercy, as He thus demonstrated in His own life-acts, saying, " The works that I do, ye shall do also."

LXXIII.

We think what we call death comes of God, our co-eternal life, when it and all its concomitants in misery—cruel lives and bitter enslaving thoughts —come of the selfish lives we lead.

We must remember these enslaved thoughts have no outgo except by their equal material direction.

Our lives are of God our Father, and not of a misery made of our own thinking.

We will find it no idle task to empty our thoughts of that in which all our lives have been spent, but we must be diligent.

Lives made up of the history of human thinking represent not God, the Author of Life.

LXXIV.

THE highest and holiest wish of man should be to keep the whole human race at heart in a bond of purity.

The waters that flow by us in the glad river and the clear bosom of the lake reflect the pure heavens above us.

We never think of the fact that water is the only thing in creation in its pure state in which we can see our faces.

If we would take this simile to our lives, the Water of the regenerating Holy Spirit would be every day a blessing to us instead of the mystery that we permit our theories to make it.

Then we could see the meaning, " Come ye to the waters," " And by water and the Holy Spirit."

We must sift these things and reason, and thus renew our lives in the Life the Master demonstrated.

Then we will lead no longer idle, supposititious lives, that show not forth the fruits of the Spirit, but move around with a new grace that is born of Life, and enjoy the treasures of the storehouse of God that is on every hand.

LXXV.

We find ourselves struggling in sickness without a friend, and we murmur and mourn.

And the doctor comes in, and we take our destiny from his expression. We have the impress of his thoughts at once that we cannot recover.

We remember in our own lives, when the doctors desired our consent to their methods of medication, we turned away, saying, " When life must go it will be in peace, and not by your ' experiments.' "

The sick are at the mercy of the doctors, and taking their decisions, find no peace for the body.

Then the spiritual doctor comes in, but the soul-body is to him invisible; yet he talks and makes statements the which his own life has not carried out.

And how could it be possible for the poor sufferer to think of these things amid so much bodily anguish ?

At times in history we are told that men refuse what is called " the comforts of religion," and it is this very thing on the part of the non-demonstrated lives of the teachers and doctors that produces unwittingly the result they would prevent.

Men say to themselves, " Their lives are as mine ; their acts are no different ; and if what they tell me is so precious, it would show forth itself in all they do, as well as what they utter with their lips only."

We can see by these things with what care we should select persons to give consolation, how their lives should show forth " that ye do justly, love mercy, and walk humbly with God."

But they do as others, yet we leave to their care the precious existence, " the express image of His Person," just as if they could take it to their own keeping.

Behold, they are the first summoned in illness and sorrow, when Jesus says, " In Me is thine help."

When if, for one moment, we could reason with our Father, we would find that He only sees us as

He made us, we would be whole just as the blind
man, whose mind caught the Light of Jesus, and
said, " This I know, that whereas I was born blind,
now I see."

The Purity of Jesus was in his mind, and he
knew that Life also was of Jesus, and his eyes
opened.

But the swine in human thought makes all appear enveloped in mystery, so we have to work
hard to realize we are the children of God.

And the world passes by on the other side in
sorrow and suffering, saying, " Send for the doctor ; that is all that can be done ;" thus we are
left in distress, to do as best we may.

LXXVI.

" As long as thou doest well to thyself, men will
think well of thee."   But the swine in human flesh
wait on us in prosperity, and as rapidly vanish
amid anguish and misfortune ; and as the slaves
of suffering press us, we struggle for freedom.

And we turn our longing gaze away from all
these in our desire of relief.

And we must be free, and lose no time in its
accomplishment.

We find the colonizing of ourselves in theory does not do the work we desire.

We still have hungry and thirsty thoughts and lives among us.

Who will come to Macedonia and help us?

We must look at the slaves of men for generations, and this will help us in thinking of Life as the free man in Christ Jesus.

The great emancipation act of President Lincoln did not set the slaves to work, nor did it give them work and take away their impressions of slavery; but "the knowledge of freedom" gave them an impetus to labor, without reference to their former masters.

And this knowledge to the time-weary slave is ours, in God our Father.

We are the children of God. We have the knowledge of this when He says, "And this is Life, and Jesus Christ, whom Thou hast sent."

LXXVII.

Thus the study of Life opens the Bible to us as plainly as we read the daily papers.

Have we not heard enough of sin and wrong?

Are we not surfeited with sorrow every day?

Surely we may be at liberty to exchange our physician! We have had enough of the theory of sin, of which the babe in the womb knows nothing, and iniquity, its counterpart.

A ship arrived at Castle Garden in the city of New York.

A ship-load of paupers!

Old men and maidens, young men and children, and wives and mothers, all in poverty of the direst sort.

The President of the United States and his Cabinet met in council.

They decided, " with one consent," " We will not have these paupers, indigent aged, and young ones as well. We have enough ; we must do our best to rid the country of such representatives." Has not the soul the right to say, We will not have these paupers of sin, sickness, and death palmed upon us of iniquity in heredity and condemnation ? We will be clean, and have done with the midnight darkness of the Egypt of self in all uncleanness !

The Life in God is ours ! The thought advanced to us in Jesus' Life is ours, and we will be weary no more, but go to Christ our Brother, and take our stand as our right of birth in the Israel of God.

Let us live to a salvation of Life, and our lives will be comforted as we grieve amid all the misfortunes by the way.

LXXVIII.

A LIFE hid with Christ in God shows forth the fruits of what our Master demonstrated.

Better by far take lessons of the bee, the bud, and the blossom than our theory-making selves.

Behold, our Father says, " Go to the ant, thou sluggard ; consider her ways, and be wise !''

Man makes his life up of theory, and gets sick and passes out of sight of his fellows ; but he, having opened his eyes on Life, is now really alive.

We see men live to eat, and eat to live ; by such monstrous misconceptions of Life, is it startling that we get sick and do what the world calls '' die'' ?

O God, our Father, what lives men live ! Yet the spires of the churches still point upward, and the congregations are at worship therein !

And they go down to their houses as usual, thinking no more of the blessings of life than they did before.

By the teachings we receive from our cradles up, is it marvellous that we suffer?

Can we wonder at anything that comes to us?

Behold families as they are reared!

Behold sorrow, sickness, suffering, and disgrace, all called the providence of God!

All this is regarded as the work of the pure and holy God!

This makes creation weep, and thick clouds of sorrow encompass us.

LXXIX.

WE attest to being Christians, and keep onward in our unholy thinking, at variance with our neighbor and ourselves! We attest to these things, and do deprive ourselves of all power to help ourselves in the midnight of bodily anguish, amid the outcries for life and its exceeding thirst for the "Water Brooks."

Soul-peace gives us bodily quiet, and we cannot argue it out of life.

LXXX.

WE cannot be too careful of our homes and the outgrowth of the family.

We send our boys from home as soon as they can get employment, and we think not of the little shielding care we have given their lives.

The boys learn material lessons. The girls are left to the care of an idle sentiment, that brings them only sorrow.

These things ought not so to be.

Would a man make a magnificent work to destroy it?

Has God made us to destroy us?

Behold, " God made man in His own image, and breathed into his nostrils the breath of life, and man became a living soul!"

What is soul?

It is beyond the power of man to explain!

Yet we say soul in body!

Yet we say body dies!

Yet we say soul lives!

And we do not say what soul is doing without its much-abused companion, body!

But we say soul has gone! Gone where?

And we say body is dead because of sin, and because of that sin it has gone out of life, and has taken the soul that is Immortal with it !

And we continue these assertions, and keeping our lives in darkness, as we insist on looking on the body as sin, and call it the habitation of the immortal soul.

A live man asleep with a body of death !

LXXXI.

IF we will draw nigh to God, we will feel that He draws nigh to us, and that " He sees us as He made us."

And we will cease to regard body a myth, barely able to be mentioned for fear some evil will step in at the suggestion.

Even the voices of our babes are hushed as they ask questions.

Mothers, take your boys and girls, and snatch them from the ignominy that your overweening delicacy brings to your lives.

If you do not tenderly tell them of life, some serpent of your society will plentifully do this for you. Thus you thrust your beautiful children into degradation by your own acts.

Thus we condemn life to a misery of our own creation, when it is a boon of God.

And if God had need to create to see us in sin and to destroy us, we are most miserable.

By this thinking we have vagrant "gods and lords many," wasting time and precious material, and we stand afar off, accusing the Giver of it all.

LXXXII.

WE wonder no more that people pass out of the body ! They get tired of living, and do not desire to continue life with its constant care, for the little tenure which theory gives is so helpless to aid, that they soon pass out of sight of material-making man.

Men firing at a target all their lives become tired, and commence a search for the object toward which all their efforts have been sent ; and finding nothing, they get dispirited, and life is a blank.

By the very call, " Come now, and let us reason together," we find in this privilege that God our Father makes us His equals.

Men do not reason with beggars, but with equals.

Suppose the Chief Justice of the United States

should call us to council ; at that moment he would recognize us as equals.

And in this call of our Father we are at once made whole in Him, and this acknowledgment of His presence takes away all Life's ills and makes us well.   And we must recognize Life in this way, or we go on in suffering.   Few think of this, and few keep it in mind after they are healed.

LXXXIII.

THE decay of humanity is frightful, but it is looked upon as natural.

And this bare supposition of its naturalness gives less power to clear away the slough of despond.

Now, what we must have is the comprehension that we came of Life, and by this fact whispered into our ears, We will help ourselves and others.

LXXXIV.

MAN is a great and blessed reality, and he must go on to conquer.

A power capable of eternal existence does not also possess a power to annihilate.

We must welcome these thoughts, and realize

error as nothing, and it will unclasp its hold on our lives !

We cannot mar the real if we would ; the Eternal Limner is the Counterpart, thus we cannot be defaced.

LXXXV.

LIFE is loaded past the gunwales with theoretical decisions.

We must unload, or sink amid disease and despair.

We must ship the old cargo material, and this will bring us to the Harbor of Life, the Orient of the Sun of Righteousness.

LXXXVI.

Joy and peace are not to be found in the self-life of mankind.

Mercy and truth meet when we bring forth the fruits of the Spirit.

And this we can do, or the words of Jesus are vain.

But behold how people cling to self, and donate to their best beloved of earth-life the eternal fires, if they do not acknowledge to a belief in a theory in which they themselves live.

LXXXVII.

The innumerable flowers of Mercy spring to life in " judge not, and ye shall not be judged."

And we must make every effort to get out of the darkness of self-life.

Over the doors of most homes is written, " This house is for me and mine."

We must open our lives to the sunlight of God, and joy and peace will spring up in the once weary, darkened homes.

LXXXVIII.

God is success ; His works prove it.

The works of our Father are all before us, and the Life of our Friend and Brother, Jesus, was a constant demonstration. Yet we turn away, saying that Jesus did not mean that we should demonstrate His Life here when He said, " The kingdom of heaven (the condition of harmony) is within you."

St. Paul says, " I was born free."

And the centurion said, " With great price purchased I this freedom."

Some of us get to the Light ; some of us wait in the byways of self, and have to work with " the great price" mentioned by the centurion, to find a glimpse of the Spirit.

But leaving self outside brings us at once to the presence of the King.

LXXXIX.

THE enslaved thought and the chained slave are both subjects of commiseration.

By ceasing to colonize man-made decisions, the hungry life realizes its Maker.

This is what we think Jesus meant in saying, " Call no man your Father upon earth, for one is your Father, even God," and when He spoke of " leaving houses and lands for My sake, and the gospel's."

In the fast-developing future people will come to the Light and to the millennium of soul.

XC.

LET us continue with unceasing avidity in search for Truth, and we will find the joy of the promise, " They that wait on the Lord shall run and not be weary ; they shall walk, and not faint."

And the Bible will be to us the Book of books, instead of a mystery.

XCI.

WE do not have " dominion" over Life because we will not leave out self, continuing as we do to insist that Jesus did not intend His demonstrated life-acts to be applied to our daily need, but to another world.

Do we know any other sphere of existence where they could be more needed ?

The chains of self-life bind us as did the ancient bond of the slave.

By a word President Lincoln set millions free. To that decree men bowed in adoration, and none more than the emancipated slave.

But in releasing the captives of sorrow, the emancipation of our lives from self, we cry out, " Oh, this cannot be here ; it is for the ' Home Over There ! ' "

But where is the day and place of soul-freedom ? And when shall we hear, " Come unto Me, and I will give you rest" ?

Do slaves in chains have this said to them of their masters ?

We can be assured we are not left alone of God, or the words and life of Jesus are but a hidden mystery, that He Himself did not explain.

When will we be free from man-made theories, that wash out all hope and bind us to sickness and sorrow?

XCII.

COULD Jesus' Love harm us?

If this could be so, we thereby make God a party to misfortune, and a looker-on of the woes Jesus came to heal.

We must realize "self-thinking" has no power to control; this will help us continue a diligent pursuit of our inheritance.

We must claim the whole of Life, not a part.

We must go forward to the Real Source, and not permit our pride and ignorance to choke the good seed.

Let us be sure to keep sin away from our lives, and then we will be present to the All-Power.

And we know we really have a Father in God, and that no power can deprive us of Him.

To this position all our lives and energies must

be bent, even though the way may seem to " be hedged in."

XCIII.

WE are assured saying prayer is the soul's sin- ceie desire does not explain what prayer is to our lives, nor what it is in substance.

We want to be free to the comprehension of " I will give you rest." We want to *know* the sub- stance of things hoped for. We want to know Spirit, and not a theory unexplainable.

We desire to know Life is ours, and realize we are drinking of the Living Waters.

We know the Eternal Presence unites man with his Maker.

Let us bravely work on, knowing evil has no ex- istence in Life, and listen to our Father's voice, calling us all the time, " It is I, be not afraid."

Then the scales will fall from our eyes, and we are made whole.

And this we do know, " and testify to what we have seen," and who can hinder our evidence ?

We have seen pitiful faces shine with the Truth that set them free in realizing their birthright of soul-purity.

Many persons say, " I cannot understand what you mean !"

Neither could those comprehend Greek or Latin who have never learned them.

If we only take lessons of self, how can we know what are the fruits of " waiting on the Lord "?

We are to remember Life is of God, and by taking ourselves to Him in the witness of the Spirit, " comes the fruits."

And we must have this, or drop by the way, eating husks, when there is " enough and to spare in our Father's house."

We must cease to give place to the devouring beasts of sickness and sorrow.

XCIV.

WE must awake to Life. You will say this is not telling us what it is to live ! Do we not feel life in every action ? Then is not this proof that we came of life and not death ?

Every action is life, yet we lay no stress thereto, but go on in our blindness, and continue saying, Life is evil, and sin is for us of God.

XCV.

WHEN sin presented itself to Jesus, He said, "Get thee behind me, Satan;" and this Satan of death robs life of its possessions by our giving intellect power and place to translate Life to convey death, thus making the demonstrated life of Jesus of no avail.

These suppositions tell us the prayer.

"Our Father was not to be our own, but the property of a statistical position, that says, We cannot cure you by asking, and there is no God that you can ask, for all Life and words of Jesus are left to us to explain; and as we cannot make your faces shine in the comfort of life, you cannot find peace yourselves, because we have it not; and what our intellect cannot attain the simple fishermen of Galilee left out of their narrative, for they were unlearned."

Parents always see their offsprings as children only. They never realize that the boy is a man, but in all instances hold them in mind as babes.

And so our Father sees us as He made us, and not as we make ourselves.

In this simplicity we realize the Eternal Source of Life.

This gives health to the bones and rest to our lives.

Was it theory that gave the martyrs comfort?

Was it the ecstasy of the hour that stayed their souls?

We do well know, in such a time nothing could comfort them but a knowledge that all is Life. And amid their flames they must have had the *knowledge* and not the supposition of Life.

Since it must have been knowledge of Eternal Life that kept the martyrs, is it not the same that drives away sin, sickness, and sorrow, and leads us to comprehend, " O Death, I will be thy plagues" ?

XCVI.

THE tyrant self slays all things, and leaves us trembling by the " roadside."

We go forth, taking life to preserve life. Behold the numbers that rush to the sea-shore and the mountains to heal life !

They have taken the privilege of life in animals, and in their nervous exhaustion from having eaten the flesh of the trembling, affrighted animal, they have to leave their elegant homes for places to recruit wasted strength.

These have no resource but to repeat the nauseous dose; thus, amid their sloth and fashion, they pass out of sight, while depending upon taking life to keep life.

"What is man?" "He is no more than the food he eats, since he obliges himself to acknowledge his dependence thereupon."

Disease and distress of all kinds can be traced in the taking of the lives of the trembling animals; yet we go on saying, we are given no power to help ourselves, and that we would be unable to live without this general slaughter of the innocent creatures in our fields.

You are ready to say, And how can we live?

XCVII.

PERHAPS in your life you may have had sorrow.

Perhaps you may have been laid up for years an helpless cripple, so dependent on others that life was a burden to you, while you, too, may have been a burden to those around you.

Perhaps you prayed, perhaps others also asked in prayer, yet no relief was vouchsafed.

At one time we heard a good, patient soul say, "We have heard that prayer for three years ; better stop now, 'Ah ! God forgot long ago.' "

This plain language, uttered in earnest from an honest heart, gave life an impetus. This made us realize something was to be done beside *words* uttered in enthusiasm and lost in theory.

The gods of fear and lords of custom take our time, and we have to attend these, therefore we cannot work in the Vineyard.

And to these "gods and lords," in their tyrannical observances, we give our best hours.

The first fresh hue of youth and the strength of all life's labor is passed in haste to gather riches and pleasures.

Riches that fade at our grasp and pleasures that open the door to sin, sickness, and sorrow !

Behold, our lives running away from the Maker of the birds, the buds, and blossoms, to the sickening thing called pleasure, instead of the Orient of Life, our Maker, and Jesus our Friend !

Now, it is said this is what the world does ; and how can it be helped ?

We hasten to extinguish fires, and to get rid of epidemics.

Have we not the means of Life at hand to escape the leprosy of sin and sickness ?

We will have a struggle, but we can awake from self to our Life in the All-Power, and will come out conquerors.

XCVIII.

WHEN a farmer clears a field, he has hard work because of the undergrowth and knotty old stumps. Yet he works with joy, for he knows the soil has life, and that it will bring a rich harvest to him.

And as we see the fair fruit of Life coming to us, let us fear no one, but regard God, who will never forsake us.

Thus holding to the Enduring, the Good, and the True, we leave " out lords many and gods many."

XCIX.

How often do we see people rush into a state of life called union that is utterly devoid of it in every instance !

Unselfish love makes unselfish lives !

By this we see how Life and its conditions are regarded and entirely absorbed.

Though we are the children of God, we do not acknowledge Him in our ways; but as the sun is hid on a day of clouds, "so gods many and lords many" hide Life from us; yet the lilies the waves have swept under are the fair lilies of the field, and so are we ever the children of God.

And we are bold enough in our human pride to place theory beside the " Ark of the Covenant."

Behold, how soon it is struck down by the knowledge of All Life!

We thus realize God our Father cannot be steadied on the sandy foundations of human thinking.

This explains to us the conversion of St. Paul, how the scales fell from his eyes.

We grasp this slowly, but it will come to us.

Most people exist upon what is called pleasure, and this failing them, they pass out to what men call death!

Behold the families of the wealthy, in their imposed misery!

We can go out from the charnel-house of man-made living to the peace of God, " who giveth to all men liberally, and upbraideth not!"

Even our daily acts and expressions awaken to remind us of God our Life.

In our routine of thought we write *AM*, and the Bright and Morning Star, I AM, is before us. "I am the Bright and Morning Star."

I AM God the Father, and Jesus thy brother, crowning all life with the rubies of sympathy and love.

From God only can come these, and not their opposite.

Behold, in our barren lives we do not even profit by what theory calls holy !

C.

AMID the homes of poverty and distress, is it startling that the helpless ones do not see Life ?

Is it any amazement the absorbed glutton, amid so-called pleaures, lives on, and the words of Life that may fall on the ear from the soft-cushioned pew in the luxurious church is not understood, and the oft-repeated tale comes to us, " They died unconverted " ?

Is it astounding that there are so few evidences of the fruits of the Spirit, while we see so many dead in luxury and self ?

And why do we complain of others while our lives are so empty !

We must have our lives as our Master showed us.

And we must show it forth by a happy result.

A life given to self is a harbor of suspicion.

We see lives thus given to self, and the eventide is but suspicion and misfortune.

Behold, every step of Jesus' life was love and sacrifice ; and how can we go on calling ourselves Christians, when we give vent to the stings of cruel suspicion and bitter enmity ? Even when we would help others, it is with a cruel stare, as much as if we would say, " Come not nigh ; I am holier than thou !"

CI.

CAN we expect to cure the sick by telling them they cannot recover ?

Can we expect a child to obey when we are ever telling it of its faults ?

We need encouragement and love, and not cold philosophy.

Let us make our lives glad and pure, as Jesus gave them back to us.

Whatever ills we have, we are the creators thereof.

First on the list of duties is Christ's law of love, and no other greater follows.

Let the tongue of suspicion cease !

Let the tongue of venom write anguish no more in any hearts !

Let life be Love ; this gives peace to the eventide.

Let us prize Life, and make it the type of our Master, and strive to a perfect union in thought, word, and deed !

Let us help all to nobly live, and show forth the endowed Life we have !

By so doing we will cease seeing ruined homes, and we will look down from the watch-tower with the powers of Life our own.

Thus Life made pure by heaven-born tenderness will show to us that God's gifts do not fetter us.

And, finally, a life rounded out in the beauty of holiness shall be recognized as the handiwork of the *Beautiful Builders.*

www.ingramcontent.com/pod-product-compliance
Lightning Source LLC
Chambersburg PA
CBHW032009010726
47493CB00007B/2331